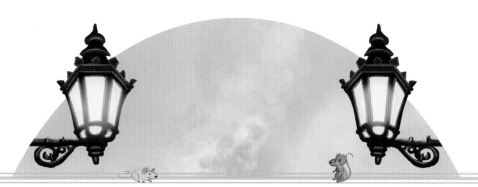

This igloo book belongs to:

....

igloobooks

*Published in 2020
by Igloo Books Ltd
Cottage Farm
Sywell
NN6 0BJ
www.igloobooks.com*

Copyright © 2018 Igloo Books Ltd
Igloo Books is an imprint of Bonnier Books UK

0620 002
2 4 6 8 10 9 7 5 3
ISBN 978-1-83903-302-5

Original story by Charles Dickens
Retold by Stephanie Moss
Illustrated by Eva Morales

Designed by Justine Ablett
Edited by Stephanie Moss

Printed and manufactured in China

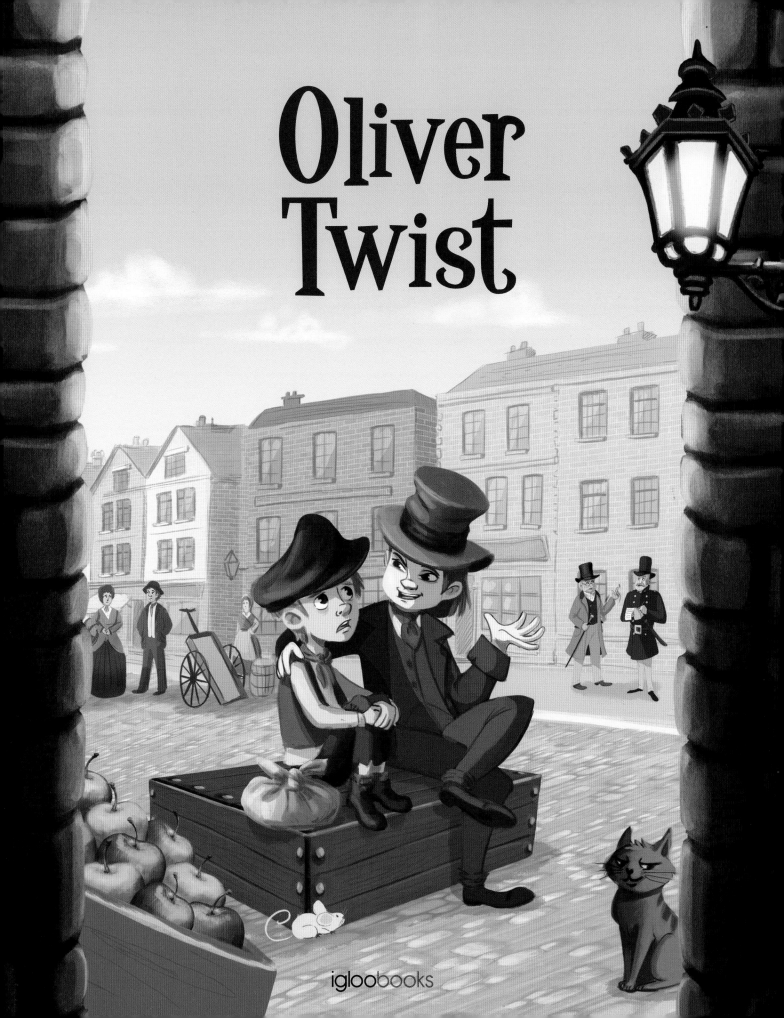

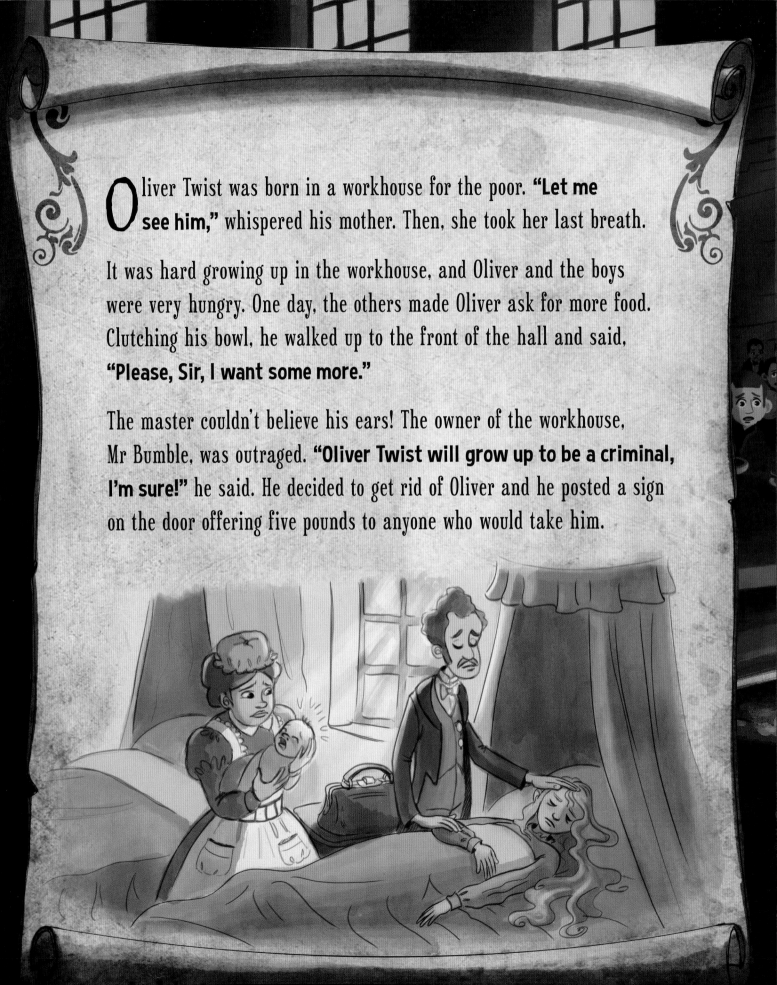

Oliver Twist was born in a workhouse for the poor. **"Let me see him,"** whispered his mother. Then, she took her last breath.

It was hard growing up in the workhouse, and Oliver and the boys were very hungry. One day, the others made Oliver ask for more food. Clutching his bowl, he walked up to the front of the hall and said, **"Please, Sir, I want some more."**

The master couldn't believe his ears! The owner of the workhouse, Mr Bumble, was outraged. **"Oliver Twist will grow up to be a criminal, I'm sure!"** he said. He decided to get rid of Oliver and he posted a sign on the door offering five pounds to anyone who would take him.

The next day, the local funeral director arrived at the workhouse. **"Hello, Mr Sowerberry,"** said Mr Bumble, with a smile on his face. **"Would you like an apprentice?"** Mr Sowerberry looked down his nose when he saw little Oliver, but he agreed.

"Look up, boy," whispered Mr Bumble, but as Oliver was led away, a single tear rolled down his cheek.

In his new home, Oliver was fed only scraps and made to sleep with the coffins. He was bullied by an older boy called Noah Claypole. **"Your mother was a bad-un, workhouse boy!"** jeered Noah. **"Shut up,"** whispered Oliver, but Noah refused. Overcome by anger, Oliver grabbed Noah and threw him to the ground.

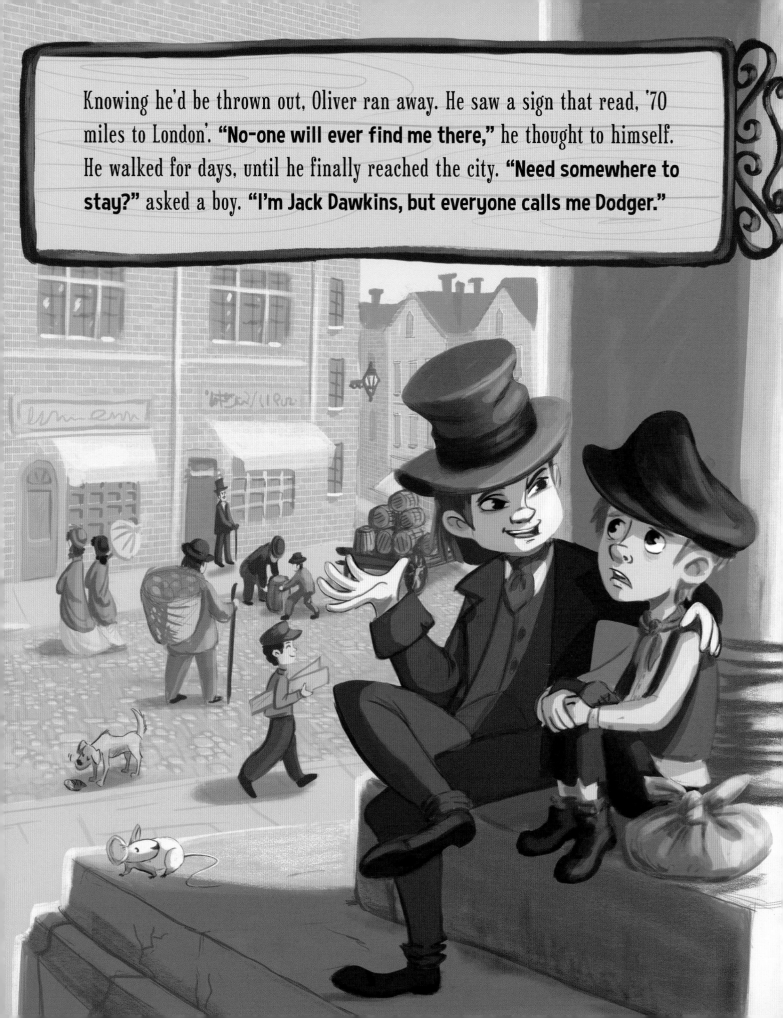

Knowing he'd be thrown out, Oliver ran away. He saw a sign that read, '70 miles to London'. **"No-one will ever find me there,"** he thought to himself. He walked for days, until he finally reached the city. **"Need somewhere to stay?"** asked a boy. **"I'm Jack Dawkins, but everyone calls me Dodger."**

Dodger led Oliver to a small room, where he met an old man called Fagin. **"Come in, my dear,"** said Fagin.

That night, Oliver slept soundly, but in the morning, he saw Fagin with handfuls of sparkling jewels. Suddenly, he noticed Oliver and whispered, **"What did you see?"** **"Nothing,"** promised Oliver, so Fagin smiled. **"Let's play a game, my dear,"** he said. **"Take this handkerchief out of my pocket without me noticing."**

Oliver was good at Fagin's game, and the next day, Dodger took him on an outing. Before long, Dodger pointed to a smart-looking old gentleman at a bookstall and said, **"That one."**
Then, Oliver watched Dodger take the man's handkerchief from his pocket and run off as quickly as he could.

"My new friends are all crooks," realised poor Oliver.

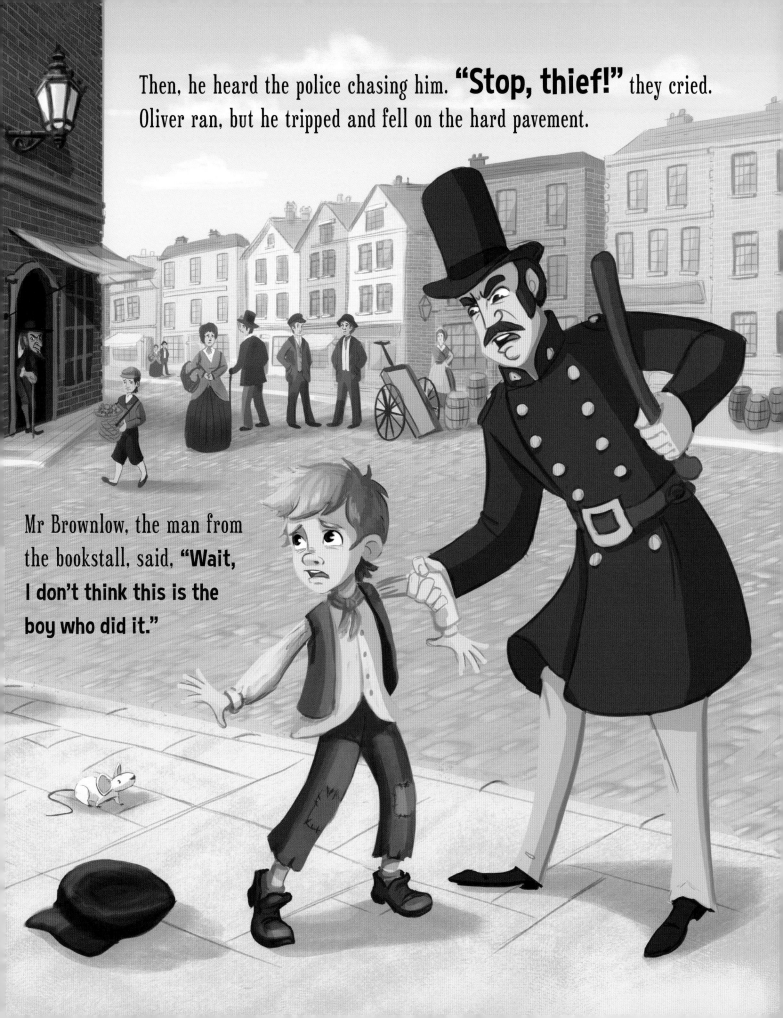

Then, he heard the police chasing him. **"Stop, thief!"** they cried.
Oliver ran, but he tripped and fell on the hard pavement.

Mr Brownlow, the man from
the bookstall, said, **"Wait,
I don't think this is the
boy who did it."**

Mr Brownlow thought he recognised Oliver. **"I must be imagining it,"** he thought, but he wanted to help. So, he asked Oliver to stay with him and the boy was overjoyed.

When Oliver explored Mr Brownlow's house, he saw a portrait of a beautiful woman. **"She looks just like me,"** he gasped.

It was wonderful living with the kind and generous Mr Brownlow, who took better care of Oliver than anyone before. One day, Mr Brownlow asked Oliver to return some books for him. He set off at once, but little did Oliver know, his old friend, Fagin, had not forgotten about him.

"Get him back!" cried Fagin. **"What if he tells the police something that will get us into trouble?"**

So, Bill Sikes, who was a robber in Fagin's gang, told his girlfriend, Nancy, to help them find out where Oliver was.

When their plan was ready, Bill and Nancy set off.

On his way to the bookstall, Oliver heard a woman screaming. Then, she ran towards him.

"Oh, my dear little brother, thank goodness I've found you!" pretended Nancy.

"Come back home," joined in Bill, as his dog, Bullseye, snarled.

"Help, I don't know them!" cried Oliver, as they dragged him away.

Fagin watched Oliver closely for days,
but Nancy was kind and grew fond of him.

One night, Sikes grabbed Oliver and dragged
him through the dark, foggy streets.
"We've got a job to do," he growled.
When they reached a grand house,
Sikes whispered, **"Climb through that
window and unlock the door."**

Oliver realised that Sikes wanted
to rob the house and he refused.
Then, Sikes pulled out a pistol.

Scared Oliver did as he was told, then suddenly Sikes shouted, **"It's the owners!"** and squeezed the trigger.

There was a

FLASH and a BANG!

Oliver cried out, as his arm started throbbing.

Sikes ran away, but Oliver couldn't keep up. Soon, Nancy found him and took him to Mr Brownlow. She knew about the robbery, so she had followed Oliver to help. Nancy and Mr Brownlow spoke quietly about a man Oliver didn't know, then Mr Brownlow said, **"I'll find him."** Nancy hurried away.

Oliver was safe with Mr Brownlow, but Sikes was furious when he found out what Nancy had done. **"Why are you looking at me like that, Bill?"** Nancy whispered. **"You betrayed me!"** he cried, and with that, Sikes raised his fist. Nancy screamed in the darkness, never to be seen again.

Everywhere he went, Sikes was haunted by his dreadful crime. On the run from the police, he heard people whispering as he lurked in the shadows.

"They haven't caught the killer yet," they said, "but the papers say Fagin's been arrested at last. He'll be in prison for life."

With Bullseye yapping at his heels, Sikes was easy to spot, so to escape the police, he climbed up a tumbledown building. Before he could jump to the next roof, someone in the crowd below called, **"There he is!"**

Sikes slipped and fell, finally paying for Nancy's life with his own.

Meanwhile, Mr Brownlow had found the mysterious man he'd spoken to Nancy about. His name was Monks and Mr Brownlow had been his father's oldest friend. All along, Monks had been secretly trying to get Oliver into trouble. Mr Brownlow tricked Monks into meeting him so he could find out the truth. **"Why did you want to ruin Oliver?"** he asked.

Monks explained that Oliver was his long-lost half-brother, but he'd asked Fagin to turn him into a criminal. **"Unless he breaks the law, we have to share the money in our father's will,"** he muttered.

Mr Brownlow let Monks go to start a new, honest life. Then, he told Oliver everything.

"My best friend gave me this before he died," said Mr Brownlow, pointing to the portrait Oliver had noticed before. "Now I know that my friend was your father and the woman in the painting is your mother, Agnes." Once Oliver knew who he really was, he felt truly happy. Mr Brownlow adopted him and they lived as a family for the rest of their days.